BEWARE OF THE BULL!

Dick King-Smith

illustrated by John Sharp

a story from the  Yorkshire Television series

HEINEMANN · LONDON

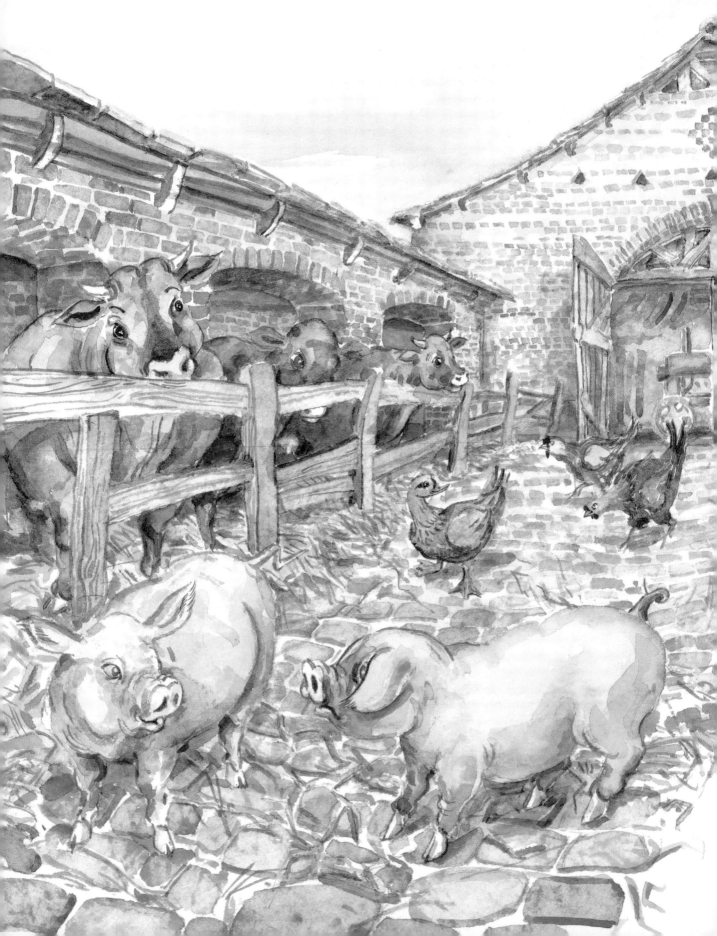

The story I've got for my granddaughter
Georgina (and you) didn't happen
here at Tumbledown Farm, but long ago.
It's a story about a bull.

Keep away from bulls.
They can be very dangerous.
I only kept away from this
one by flying like a bird.

It happened at a farm sale.

First to be sold were the implements,
like ploughs and harrows and
rollers, and the machines.

There was an old tractor there,
just like Fred Fordson.

Then the auctioneer sold the pigs

and the ducks and geese

and the sheep

and chickens.

There were some hens that looked
very like the Chickabiddies.

Then he sold the cows
and, last of all, the bull.

The bull was kept in a dark shed, and
didn't come out into the daylight very often.

Now a man brought the bull out,
on a bull-pole attached to the ring in his nose.
The bull blinked in the sunshine
and stared at all the people.

"Now then, gentlemen!" shouted the auctioneer.
"What am I bid for this fine young bull?
Quiet as a lamb, he is."

But the bull wouldn't go into the sale-ring.

"Bring him along!" shouted the auctioneer.
And some silly person gave the bull
a whack with a stick.

And he jumped forward.
And the bull-pole broke.

Everybody scattered!
Into sheds they went,
and on to waggons,
and even up ladders.

Only one person still stood there,
as the bull trotted into the sale-ring.

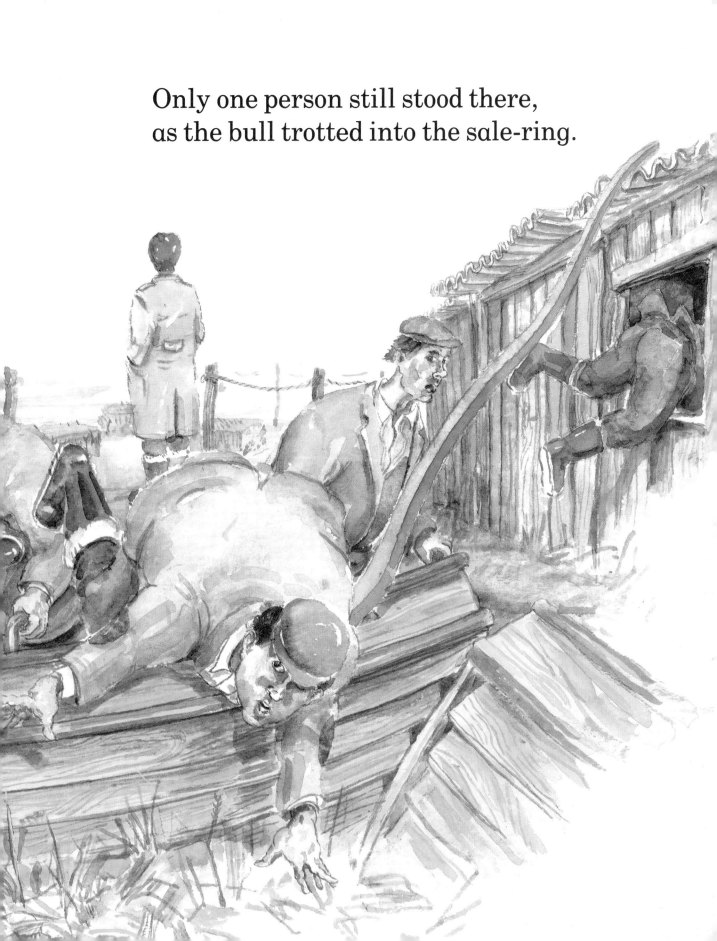

I was daydreaming, you see. I was dreaming about the time when I would have my own farm,

with my own tractor,

and my own animals.

And then I looked round
and I couldn't see anyone.
The sale must be over, I thought.
They've all gone home. I'm all alone.

But I wasn't.

There was the bull, right in front of me,
with only a few straw bales between us!

And he didn't look very pleased.
He pawed the ground and snorted.

For a moment neither of us moved.
Then the bull put his head down and charged.
And then – for the first and only time –
I flew through the air like a bird.

A big clumsy bird,
wearing a heavy old army
greatcoat and wellies!

I flew so fast that I hit
a nearby gate-post and snapped
it off like a carrot!

And the bull thundered past me
and galloped off across the fields.

And I picked myself up. And everybody
came out of their hiding-places.
So just remember –

Beware of the Bull!

First published 1989 by William Heinemann Ltd

Text © Fox Busters Ltd 1989
Illustrations © Yorkshire Television Ltd 1989
Television Programme © Yorkshire Television 1988
Executive Producer: Chris Jelley
Director: Don Clayton
Associate Producer: Sally Wells
Producer: Michael Harris

William Heinemann Ltd.
Michelin House
81 Fulham Road, London SW3 6RB

ISBN (hardback) 434 94628 1
    (paperback) 434 94626 5

Printed by MacLehose and Partners Ltd
in Great Britain